Ella and One Big Dream
Text and Illustrations by: C. L. Fails

© 2017 LaunchCrate Publishing

LaunchCrate Publishing
info@launchcrate.com
www.launchcrate.com

Ordering Information:
Quantity sales. Special discounts are available on quantity purchases by corporations, associations, and others. For details, contact the publisher at the email address above. Orders by U.S. trade bookstores and wholesalers.

Library of Congress Control Number: 2017916951

ISBN: 978-1-9475060-7-7

Printed in the United States of America
10 9 8 7 6 5 4 3 2 1

First Edition

May your dreams be grand and your chase be full
of adventures...

The children gathered on the floor.
Ms. Ann sat in front, to read once more.

"Story hour has begun. Books for all, then books for one!" said Ms. Ann with a smile.

"Are you ready?" sang Ms. Ann.

"Yes we are!" their chant began.

"On the floor with legs tucked in, let our storytime begin!"

So what's the story of the day?

"*Ducks Don't Drum,*" they heard her say.

The children giggled with bellies full of silly flies.

With eyes locked on the storybook, Ms. Ann nodded with a look.

"Turn on your Imagicap!"
CLICK - BUZZ - CRACKLE - SPARK - ZZZZZZAP

It was all warmed up and ready to think,
but Ella's Imagicap must have been on the brink.
Ready for a funny tale,
she waited and waited, to no avail.

Using a QR Code reader, scan this page to read,
"Ducks Don't Drum."

Ms. Ann finished reading, but the book was so glum.
"Ducks don't drum? Why not? How come?"
Ms. Ann smiled wide and clapped with zest
while Ella's questions would not rest.

The class was polled about their dreams.
Their little eyes shined all agleam.

Hand after hand burst up with pride,
waving front to back and side to side.

Doctor! Policeman! Librarian! Writer!
Chef! Actor! Singer! Firefighter!

They "oohed," and "ahhed," with each passing craft,
but soon things shifted and all the kids laughed.

Why?

Ella joined in with full sound effects,
"Augmented Reality Architect!"

"A WHOOSIE WHAT?" someone asked, funny faced.
"A-moogly ra-toogly pakashmeck," one joked in bad taste.

Ella's Mom knew that face
all too well.
Her big bubbly light was
crawling back in her shell.

Ms. Ann smiled at Ella and repeated her choice,
"Augmented Reality Architects need your voice!"

Holding up "Ducks Don't Drum," for all to see,
Ms. Ann asked the children to repeat with glee,

"Books for all, now books for one.
Our solo time has just begun."

The children each joined hands
with their family and rushed
to find a nook to discuss the
book...

Ella's mom softly patted her back,
"So ducks don't drum, but they thwack
when they quack!"
A smile started to rise on her cheeks
but soon faded.
The other kids' laughter had left her jaded.

"What's got you down?" asked mom with a frown.

"Well, their dreams are all cool, and I feel like a clown!"

"How about a french
fry laying there on
your plate?"

"What?"

"They don't compare their size
and they all taste great!"

Mom could see the wheels turning in Ella's head.
"I think I get it," young Ella said.

"Now what do you see when
you close your eyes?"

"One big mountain and
clouds zooming by!"

"And what do you see on the mountain top?"

"It's too high up! I can't see it," she stopped.

Mom passed her a pair of invisible goggles.
Ella strapped them on her head
and proceeded to joggle.

"Tune in," says mom, with a sly foxish smile.

"I see it!" gasps Ella, fake-turning a dial.

"It's me with goggles for all of the others.
For fathers, and sisters, and brothers, and mothers!
Everyone's viewing their biggest dream yet.
Since they can't see each others, they'll never forget!"

Ella hugged mom and giggled, with pencil in hand.
Ms. Ann passed her some paper.
She started to plan.

"Now go map your way there, my ambitious girl!
Hold on to YOUR dream and go conquer the world!"

CPSIA information can be obtained at www.ICGtesting.com
Printed in the USA
LVIW01n0739281117
557855LV00026B/503